Penguin Books

THE PENGUIN BOOK
OF ENGLISH MADRIGALS:
FOR FOUR VOICES

Denis Stevens, founder-conductor of the Ambrosian Consort and the Accademia Monteverdiana, was educated at Oxford, London, and Paris – combining interests in languages, musicology, and chamber music. He specialized in medieval, Renaissance, and baroque programmes during his five years as a producer in the B.B.C. Music Division in London, which he left in 1954 for his first visiting professorship in the United States. After fulfilling invitations to Cornell University, the University of California at Berkeley, and Pennsylvania State University, he was Professor of Musicology at Columbia University in New York City from 1964 to 1974, and was then appointed Distinguished Professor at Pennsylvania State University and at the University of Washington in Seattle. He has also been a visiting professor to the University of Michigan and the San Diego State University. Apart from his academic and literary work, he has edited much early music, made many records whose repertoire ranges from plainchant to Beethoven, and has also appeared with his musicians in European and American festivals as well as on radio and television. His books include *A History of Song*, *Tudor Church Music*, *Thomas Tomkins*, *Claudio Monteverdi: Sacred, Secular, and Occasional Music*, *The Letters of Monteverdi*, *Renaissance Dialogues*, *The Worcester Fragments* and (with Alec Robertson) *The Pelican History of Music*. He is also editor of *The Second Penguin Book of English Madrigals: For Five Voices*.

THE PENGUIN BOOK OF

English Madrigals

FOR FOUR VOICES

EDITED BY
DENIS STEVENS

PENGUIN BOOKS

PENGUIN BOOKS

Published by the Penguin Group
27 Wrights Lane, London w8 5TZ, England
Viking Penguin Inc., 40 West 23rd Street, New York, New York 10010, USA
Penguin Books Australia Ltd, Ringwood, Victoria, Australia
Penguin Books Canada Ltd, 2801 John Street, Markham, Ontario, Canada L3R 1B4
Penguin Books (NZ) Ltd, 182–190 Wairau Road, Auckland 10, New Zealand

Penguin Books Ltd, Registered Offices: Harmondsworth, Middlesex, England

First published 1967
Reprinted 1969, 1971, 1972, 1975, 1977, 1979, 1982, 1983, 1988

Printed and bound in Great Britain by
Cox & Wyman Ltd, Reading

CONTENTS

FOR
ALEC ROBERTSON
on his seventy-fifth birthday

EDITORIAL PRINCIPLES

*. . . and likewise you shall be perfectly
understood of the auditor what you sing,
which is one of the highest degrees of
praise which a musician in dittying can
attain unto or wish for.* (Thomas Morley)

A choral group, perhaps, consisting mainly of amateur singers devoted to the madrigal and to comparable vocal forms and styles; or a group of soloists, working together towards great perfection but little reward, other than a purely musical one – no matter what way we hear madrigals performed, the most impressive, delightful, and memorable interpretations are those which breathe spontaneity of a completely natural and unaffected kind. As in so many musics, the art of madrigal singing thrives upon the concealment of art, so that very often the most natural and convincing effects derive from some hidden artifice, whose secret resides in experience, learning, intuition, or an amalgam of all three.

Given a generous allowance of years, experience emerges from practical pursuits, and learning from theoretical; but intuition, born of itself, cannot be commanded to appear, and it is the one ingredient of a fine performance that defies analysis and disarms criticism. Yet there is so much to be absorbed at the lower levels of technical accomplishment that it seems only right, in a brief exposition of editorial methods, to lay more stress upon matters lying nearly within our grasp; and it can hardly be denied that the most useful pre-requisite for a vital re-creation of early music is a text at one and the same time reliable and imaginative.

Music printers in sixteenth-century England were not always reliable, and even when proofs were corrected by unusually careful and conscientious composers, the possibility of error could not be entirely ruled out. But if the great majority of printed madrigals make good musical sense most of the time, the artistic sensibility characteristic of the finest underlay of text to music frequently leaves much to be longed for. Composers relied upon singers to adjust syllables to notes in a manner satisfactory to all concerned. Four hundred years ago, singers were used to such things, just as they were used to part-books bearing only isolated strands of a polyphonic web. Modern singers need scores; and they also need guidance in the matter of text underlay if the original source is at all doubtful or corrupt. These and related topics now call for our attention.

'The individual vocal ranges of some Elizabethan madrigals pre-suppose a compass of enviable elasticity resulting perhaps from such social forms of encouragement described in Claude Hollybande's *The French Schoolemaister*, published in 1573:

Roland, shall we have a song?'

'Yea Sir: where be your books of music? for they be the best corrected.'

'They be in my chest: Katherin, take the key of my closet – you shall find them in a little till at the left hand: behold, there be fair songs at four parts.'

'Who shall sing with me?'

'You shall have company enough: David shall make the bass, John the tenor, and James the treble.'

'Begin! James, take your tune! Go to: for what do you tarry?'

'I have but a rest.'

'Roland, drink afore you begin, you will sing with a better courage.'

'It is well said: give me some white wine – that will cause me to sing better.'

'You must drink some green wine!'

'Yea, truly, to cause me to lose my voice.'

'Oh, see what a funnel, for he hath poured a quart of wine without any taking of his breath.'

Notice that the treble or soprano part is taken not by the lady of the house but by James, probably a choirboy; notice too that the wine-bibber, Roland, is the alto or counter-tenor of this group. By the simple and simultaneous act of whetting his courage and wetting his whistle, he is ready to tackle those low D's more suited to a tenor, or those high E's within the province of a treble.

In the present selection of madrigals, extremes of tessitura have been purposely avoided, so that a normal vocal quartet can be assured of the following ranges:

Ex. 1

It would have been possible to include other works by subjecting them to transposition, but the very sight of a madrigal in the key of B flat minor or F sharp major has been known to strike cheerless chill in the hearts of even the doughtiest singers. Later volumes in this series may experiment along these lines, keeping within the bounds of two flats or two sharps in the key-signature; but for the present purposes non-transposition and medium range have been the guiding principles, and will help to avoid very low notes and very high ones, which Thomas Morley likened respectively to 'a kind of humming' and 'a constrained shrieking'. In some instances, uncomfortable ranges may be avoided by exchanging parts, but the result inevitably alters the tonal balance and has consequently been used in only one madrigal, Byrd's *This sweet and merry month*, a gem that we could ill afford to lose.

Tonality is such an outstanding characteristic of the madrigalian repertoire that it seems both logical and practical to employ modern key-signatures. Bateson's *Down from above* appears in the original part-books with no key-signature, but the profusion of F sharps and the frequent as well as final cadencing on G tell us that the simplest solution to the problem is the use of a G major key-signature. Bennett's *O sleep, fond fancy*, is just as clearly in G minor, and so the old signature of one flat has been replaced (with, of course, the necessary internal adjustments) by the modern key-signature of two flats. This principle has been followed throughout the volume, except in a rare instance of quasi-modality – Morley's exquisite pair of madrigals *Now is the gentle season* and *The fields abroad*.

One particular feature of the original part-books has been deliberately and consistently heeded, and that is the exclusion of tempo and dynamic markings. Freshness and spontaneity in performance are sometimes due to a feeling among the singers that they have made a personal contribution to the latent expressive powers of the music, and it is good that they or their director should be able to mould an interpretation after their own ideas, rather than slavishly follow the dynamic drop-pings of some pedantic editor. One recalls the school hymn written by the Head-master and set to music by Dr Jolly in Aldous Huxley's *Antic Hay*:

> *(f)* For slack hands and *(dim.)* idle minds
> *(mf)* Mischief still the Tempter finds.
> *(ff)* Keep him captive in his lair;
> *(f)* Work will bind him. *(dim.)* Work is *(pp)* prayer.

Terrace-dynamics of this kind militate against the splendid subtleties of the madri-gal and clamp its emotional promise in the strait-jacket of unimaginative reproduc-tion. Let the artists decide for themselves how fast or how slow, how loud or how soft they intend to sing; but let them do so after reading the poem, which is printed here in full before the music begins.

There is, alas, one persuasive and all-pervading characteristic of the part-books that cannot be reproduced – the uninhibited free flow of notes and text without bar lines of any kind. As soon as polyphony is put into score, bar-lines become essential for modern singers and directors, and have in fact been used since the time of the earliest Renaissance scores. Although it is worth remembering that medieval scores disdained bar-lines, relying on rough-and-ready alignment combined with mensural practice to convince singers of their efficacy, a return to this ideal seems out of the question. If modern bar-lines provide welcome orientation, they do so because of their reliability and regularity. Cross-rhythms inherent in the music should not be permitted to dictate fancy barring, except when the shift in stress applies to all voice-parts.

Accordingly, in this edition, barring has been maintained with as much regularity as seems consistent with the style of the music. When individual voice-parts go their own way rhythmically (as they often do) no attempt has been made to mark the music with accents, since these invariably correspond to natural stresses of the verse or of the words themselves. If each poem is read carefully before rehearsal begins, there should be no difficulty in sustaining natural verbal accents at all times and in all voice-parts. For similar reasons, normal tied notes have been preferred to archaic practices involving dots placed to the right of bar-lines. It should not be necessary in this day and age to remind performers that bar-lines do not always coincide with stress or accent. When there is a clear metrical change, however, the nature and extent of this is indicated in order to distinguish between a mensural shift (Byrd, *This sweet and merry month*, bars 27/28) and one that appears as a result of textual accents (Farmer, *A little pretty bonny lass*, bars 17/18).

Texts have been modernized and punctuated in order to assist interpreters in every possible way, for notwithstanding the variable qualities of English madrigal poetry, the sense of the composition as a whole should emerge clearly in any per-formance worthy of the name. Capital letters are used to indicate the beginning of a new line in the original poem, since very frequently composers take liberties in setting verse and consequently obscure the underlying structure.

A new feature of this edition will, it is hoped, improve at one and the same time clarity in harmony, declamation, and form. The early part of this introduction hinted at the generally casual attitude towards refinements in both composition and proof-reading as practised in Elizabethan times, and since so many important characteristics of the madrigal are adversely affected by cavalier treatment of this kind, an attempt has been made to incorporate as an editorial method a consistent plan which the present writer has used with success over a number of years.

The first principle is to ensure that musical homophony is matched where appropriate by verbal homophony, all voice-parts singing the same syllables more or less exactly aligned. The more sensitive composers seek this effect as a matter of course, changing the order of words where necessary in order to achieve clarity of declamation. In Bateson's *Down from above*, the third line of the poem begins 'She starts thereat', and this order of words is followed by soprano and bass. Alto and tenor, entering at a different point, reverse the order to 'Thereat she starts', which aligns the words without obscuring the sense:

Ex. 2

In Farnaby's *The curtain drawn*, there is an obvious pairing of voice-parts in bars 17-19 (in spite of the trio entry in bar 16) and the bass text has therefore been altered from the original and aligned to that of the tenor. Similarly, Morley's *Die now my heart* presents a muddled example of underlay in the original version at bars 90/91, but if the alto and tenor are brought into line with soprano and bass, the result is clear and unequivocal.

Another type of adjustment, minor in fact but major in its importance for ease of breathing and accuracy of ensemble, is the regularizing of cadences in so far as the length of their final chord is concerned. In this respect many composers are careful, but not sufficiently so for an entirely satisfactory solution to the problems raised. The original notation of bar 35 in Bennett's *O sleep, fond fancy* is as follows:

Ex. 3

Soprano, tenor, and bass all hold their note to the end of the bar, since all have a rest of some sort before the beginning of the next phrase, 'Sleep, sleep, I say'; but the alto must begin this phrase on the very first beat of bar 36, and so his breathing space is neatly sliced from bar 35. This pragmatic approach nevertheless falls short of idealism, for three reasons. First, the rather audible ending 'st' of 'desirest' is heard twice in bar 35 – once when the alto finishes, and once again when the other three voice-parts finish. Second, when the alto stops singing, the spacing of the chord changes, and four-part harmony gives way suddenly to three-part. Third, the final 'st' of bar 35 is followed at once by a word whose opening sound is also sibilant, the aural effect being something like: 'desir*est*sleep'. One answer to the dilemma would be a pause on the bar-line. The solution adopted here, and at comparable points in other madrigals, is to standardize the length of the final chord, compromising between two beats in the alto and four beats in the other parts. All sing a dotted minim, which serves to bring the final 'st' in line and allow for a breath before the word 'Sleep'.

Occasionally a note has been clipped for harmonic reasons. There is a passage in Farnaby's *Construe my meaning* where a soprano note sustained for the written length would imply a discord in the second half of the bar:

Ex. 4

In the present edition, the soprano C has been changed to a minim. It could have been further trimmed to a crochet, but since the end vowel corresponds to that of the next word ('-ing / Still') there is no great harm done in leaving the C as a link between one phrase and another, the basic chord simply changing from major to minor. In Morley's *Say, gentle nymphs* we have an example of a sustained bass note which gives the effect of a momentary 6/4 chord; and later in the same madrigal a cadence in which three notes of a four-note chord (even when it changes position half-way through the bar) coincide on D.

Ex. 5

If the bass G in bar 13 is changed to a minim, the harmony reverts to normal; and when the soprano and bass D's are halved in bar 33, the alto-tenor entry sounds much clearer. On the other hand, it is not advisable to shorten the semibreve A's in bars 35 and 38 of the tenor part, since both places require that note for reasons of balance and fullness of sound.

It would be pedantic if every single instance of adjustment were made the occasion for a footnote, and in any event the prime purpose of this edition is a practical one. If performers feel that these editorial practices have been carried too far, all they have to do is to lengthen notes that feel uncomfortably short. But I do not think this very likely; and I have never experienced any objection from singers, who are only too willing as a rule to find new and artistic ways to unify breathing, phrasing, and declamation. To the members of my Ambrosian Consort (who have recorded some of these madrigals on HMV Mono HQM 1080 and Stereo HQS 1080) I extend my sincere thanks for many happy years of experiment and co-operation, and if the results as printed here add to the general pleasure of madrigal singing and eventually call for further volumes in this series, my hopes to extend and renew a most delectable form of vocal chamber music will not be in vain.

DENIS STEVENS

DOWN FROM ABOVE

THOMAS BATESON

> Down from above falls Jove in rain
> Into fair Danaë's lap amain,
> She starts thereat, yet lamblike still
> At last performeth all his will.
> Both high and low such golden gifts
> Will put their conscience to the shift.

Madrigals I à 3, 4, 5, 6 (1604), ix
To those complaining of the shortness of most madrigals, answer should be given that a steady tempo helps matters amazingly. Bateson's witty setting of this fragment of Greek legend deserves to unravel itself at a leisurely pace, which may be fixed with reference to bar 12. The word 'still' in bars 18 and 20 implies quietness as well as immobility, so that the entire phrase could be sung softly. Danaë, of course, was the daughter of Acrisius, King of Argos. On hearing that she would bear a son destined to slay him, Acrisius shut her up in a chamber of stone or brass. Jove, disguised as a shower of gold, made her the mother of Perseus who grew up to manhood and fulfilled the prophecy by accidentally killing his grandfather with a discus.

14

15

gifts, Will put their con - science to the shift, will put their

gifts, Will put their con - science to the shift, will put their

gifts, Will put their con -

gifts, Will put their con - science

con - science to the shift, will put their con - science to the

con - science to the shift, will put their con - science to the

- science to the shift, will put their con - science

to the shift,

shift, will put their con - science to the _____

shift, will put their con - science to the

to the shift, will put their con - science to the

will put their con - science to the

shift, their con - science to the shift.

shift, their con - science to the shift.

shift, their con - science to the shift.

shift, their con - science to the shift.

2   IF LOVE BE BLIND

THOMAS BATESON

If Love be blind, how hath he then the sight
   With beauty's beams my careless heart to wound?
Or, if a boy, how hath he then the might
   The mightiest conquerors to bring to ground?
O no, he is not blind, but I that lead
   My thoughts the ways that bring to restless fears;
Nor yet a boy, but I, that live in dread
   Mixed with hope, and seek for joy in tears.

Madrigals I à 3, 4, 5, 6 (1604), xi

Note that only the accent, not the metre, must change between bars 7 and 13. A repeated phrase such as 'how hath he then the might' is useful in building to a climax, the crucial word being 'conquerors'. The sense of the final section lies in the contrast between Cupid and the poet-lover: Cupid is not blind, but I am – he is not a boy, but I am.

sight, With beau – ty's beams my care – less heart to wound, to

sight, With beau – ty's beams my care – less heart _____ to wound, to

sight, With beau – ty's beams my care – less heart to wound, to

sight, With beau – ty's

wound, my care – less heart to wound, my care-less heart to

wound, my care – less heart to wound, my care – less heart to ___

wound, my care – less heart to

wound, my care – less heart to wound, my care – less heart to

beams my care – less heart to wound, my care – less heart to

wound? Or, if a boy, or, if a boy, how hath he then the

wound? Or, if a boy, or, if a boy,

wound? Or, if a boy, how hath he then the

wound? Or, if a boy,

might, the might, how hath he then the might,

how hath he then the might, how

how hath he then the might, the

might, how hath he then the might, the

how hath he then the might, how

30

O no, he is not

blind, but I that lead, O no, he is not

blind, but I that lead

O no, he is not blind, but I that

blind, but I that lead My thoughts the

blind, but I that lead My thoughts the ways that bring to

My thoughts the ways that bring to rest - less

lead, but I that lead My

35

ways that bring to rest - less fears, that bring to rest - less

rest - less fears, my thoughts the ways that bring to rest - less

fears, my thoughts the ways that bring to rest - less

thoughts the ways that bring to rest - less fears;

40

fears; Nor yet a boy, but

fears; Nor yet a boy, but

fears; Nor yet a boy, nor yet a boy, but

Nor yet a boy, nor yet a boy, but

20

3 PHYLLIS, FAREWELL

THOMAS BATESON

Phyllis, farewell, I may no longer live;
Yet if I die, fair Phyllis, I forgive.
I live too long; come, gentle death and end
My endless torment, or my grief amend.

Madrigals I à 3, 4, 5, 6 (1604), xii
Alfredo Obertello, in his valuable study of madrigal texts (*Madrigali Italiani in Inghilterra*, Milan, 1949), finds that this lyric has certain definite Italian features. The music, in contrast, has more affinity with the canzonet than with the madrigal, and the pervading touch of artless simplicity should be brought out in rehearsal and played down in performance. The phrase beginning on the last beat of bar 18 should be carried through bar 20/21 to maintain the sense. A quick breath can be taken after 'torment'.

23

4

WHITHER SO FAST?

THOMAS BATESON

> Whither so fast? See how the kindly flowers
> > Perfume the air, and all to make thee stay.
> The climbing woodbind clipping all these bowers,
> > Clips thee likewise for fear thou pass away.
> > Fortune our friend, our foe will not gainsay.
> Stay but awhile; Phoebe no tell-tale is,
> She her Endymion, I'll my Phoebe kiss.

Madrigals I à 3, 4, 5, 6 (1604), vii
This is the first verse of a poem set in full by Pilkington in his *First Book of Songs or Airs* (1605), where the final couplet appears as a refrain in all three verses. The second verse, with some alterations, appears as a madrigal in Pilkington's first set (1613). Bateson's treatment of the pastoral is full of delicate pictorial touches, and may have been conceived as a tribute to Dowland, whose *Lachrymae* motto appears at the opening and at bar 28.

thou pass a way. For-tune our

fear. thou pass a way. For - tune our

fear thou pass a - - way.

fear thou pass a - - way.

friend, For - tune our friend, our foe will not gain-

friend, For - tune our friend, our

For - tune our friend, our foe will not gain -

Our foe will not gain -

say, our foe will not gain - say.

foe will not gain - say, not gain say. Stay

say, our foe will not gain - say. Stay

say, will not gain - say.

Stay but a - - while; Phoe - be no

but a - while; but a - while; Phoe - be no

but a - while; Phoe - be no

Stay but a - while;

27

5   O SLEEP, FOND FANCY

JOHN BENNETT

O sleep, O sleep, fond fancy,
My head, alas, thou tirest,
With false delight of that which thou desirest.
Sleep, sleep, I say, fond fancy
And leave my thoughts molesting,
Thy master's head hath need of sleep and resting.

Madrigals à 4 (1599), xii

All voices share a middle-to-low tessitura contributing to a total effect of restraint and quietude, so that the opening and closing sections can be sung in a natural and unforced manner, tonally intense but dynamically fairly even. The middle section (bars 25-35) calls for a more animated approach, but this should not be allowed to intrude too much upon the prevailing atmosphere. Morley's setting of this text (in his *Plain and Easy Introduction*) may well have prompted Bennett's memorable and expressive version appearing only two years later.

6   WEEP, O MINE EYES

JOHN BENNETT

> Weep, O mine eyes, and cease not,
> Alas, these your springtides, methinks, increase not.
> O when, O when begin you
> To swell so high that I may drown me in you?

Madrigals à 4 (1599), xiii

Faced with such a poem, Bennett could hardly avoid referring to the melody of Dowland's *Lachrymae*, yet the disarmingly passionate plea brings forth a setting whose sensitivity is characteristic of Bennett alone. As his admirer Ravenscroft said (preface to the *Brief Discourse*): 'the very life of that passion, which the ditty sounded, is so truly expressed, as if he had measured it alone by his own soul, and invented no other harmony than his own sensible feeling in that affection did afford him'.

36

7 YE RESTLESS THOUGHTS

JOHN BENNETT

Ye restless thoughts, that harbour discontent,
Cease your assaults, and let my heart lament,
And let my tongue have leave to tell my grief,
That she may pity, though not grant relief.
Pity would help, alas, what Love hath almost slain,
And salve the wound that festered this disdain.

Madrigals à 4 (1599), ix

Both music and text should be allowed to flow along naturally until the cadence at 'though not grant relief', where experiment will help to determine the best way of hinting at the full stop and fresh material in the final couplet. Both this and the previous poem were set by Wilbye in his *Madrigals I à 3, 4, 5, 6* of 1598.

38

let my heart la – ment, and let my heart la –

let my heart la – ment, and let my heart la –

– saults and let my heart la – ment, and

– saults and let my heart la – ment, and

– ment, la – ment, And let my tongue

– – – ment, la – ment, And let my tongue and

let my heart la – ment, And, let my

let my heart la – ment, And let my

have leave to tell my

let my tongue have leave to tell my

tongue have leave to tell my

tongue have leave to tell my

grief, That

grief, That she may pi – ty,

grief, That she may pi – ty, though not grant re –

grief, That she may pi – ty, though not grant re –

8 THIS SWEET AND MERRY MONTH

WILLIAM BYRD

This sweet and merry month of May,
   While nature wantons in her prime,
And birds do sing, and beasts do play
   For pleasure of the joyful time,
I choose the first for holiday
   And greet Eliza with a rhyme:
O beauteous Queen of second Troy,
Take well in worth a simple toy.

Italian Madrigals Englished (1590), viii
Psalms, Songs, and Sonnets (1611), ix

This poem has been attributed to Thomas Watson, compiler of the *Italian Madrigals Englished*, whose two purely native products were Byrd's settings for four and six voices of this obviously occasional piece. The four-part setting was later reprinted in Byrd's 1611 collection. It has been suggested that one or the other version was sung at Elvetham in 1591, when Lord Hertford entertained Queen Elizabeth, but the date of first publication suggests an earlier occasion for the actual première. Byrd demonstrates with masterly ease his complete understanding of the Italian vein, and care should be exercised to bring out the apt contrasts of mood and measure that place this musical gem so firmly in the memory. For reasons of range, alto and tenor voices have been exchanged between bars 68 and 73, so that some adjustments in timbre and weight of tone may prove necessary.

45

A LITTLE PRETTY BONNY LASS

JOHN FARMER

A little pretty bonny lass was walking
  In midst of May before the sun 'gan rise.
I took her by the hand and fell to talking
  Of this and that, as best I could devise.
I swore I would, yet still she said I should not
Do what I would, and yet for all I could not.

Madrigals à 4 (1599), xiv
The speed is to some extent determined by the ability of the singers to deal with the tongue-twister in bars 35-37, *poco staccato*. Loss of clarity will effectively blunt the edge of the poet's coyly audacious wit.

FAIR PHYLLIS

JOHN FARMER

Fair Phyllis I saw sitting all alone,
  Feeding her flock near to the mountain side.
The shepherds knew not whither she was gone
  But after her lover Amyntas hied.
Up and down he wandered whilst she was missing;
  When he found her, O, then they fell a-kissing.

Madrigals à 4 (1599), xv
Farmer's original note-values are slightly unfair to the fair Phyllis, and the repeated opening phrase has therefore been modified to help both declamation and breathing.

55

57

II TAKE TIME WHILE TIME DOTH LAST

JOHN FARMER

Take time while time doth last;
Mark how fair fadeth fast;
Beware if envy reign;
Take heed of proud disdain.
Hold fast now in thy youth;
Regard thy vowed truth;
Lest when thou waxeth old
Friends fail and love grows cold.

Madrigals à 4 (1599), xvi
Taking his cue from the pun on 'time', Farmer offers here a vocal equivalent of the hexachord fantasia, and in view of the speculative nature of the interdependent words and music, a firm and deliberate tempo should be adopted.

61

63

AY ME, POOR HEART!

GILES FARNABY

Ay me, poor heart!
Since Love hath played his part,
My senses are all lost,
My mind eke tossed
Like waves that swell.
Sweet god of Love,
Thou dost excel!
Thy passions move
My mind to prove
That turtle dove.
She flies; my love she tries.
Help, gods that sit on high!
O, send me remedy.

Canzonets à 4 (1598), xv
This is an adaptation of a song for solo soprano and three viols, and there is no harm done if
some prominence is given to the uppermost line even in this madrigalian version. To avoid
the threefold repetition of the same phrase in the alto between bars 51 and 54 the middle
statement has been given to the soprano. Farnaby's own keyboard elaboration may be found in
the *Fitzwilliam Virginal Book*, ii, 330.

13 CONSTRUE MY MEANING

GILES FARNABY

Construe my meaning, wrest not my method;
Good will craves favour, witness the high God.
If I have meant well, good will reward me;
When I deserve ill, no man regard me.
What shall I say more? speech is but blasting.
Still will I hope for life everlasting.

Canzonets à 4 (1598), xx
Farnaby, who obtained an Oxford B.Mus. in 1592, seems not to have bothered over much
with the more formal regulations of academic part-writing, but the odd soprano line in bars
17/18 may be the result of an attempt to avoid fifths between the soprano and tenor. They are
however just avoided by the tenor's tied E. This faintly enigmatic text apparently tempted
Farnaby into unusual realms of tonality, and special attention must be given to intonation and
to the careful maintaining of pitch throughout.

14   SOMETIME SHE WOULD

GILES FARNABY

Sometime she would, and sometime not;
   The more request, the more disdained.
Each woman hath her gift, God wot,
   And ever had since Venus reigned.
Though Vulcan did to Venus yield,
   I would have men to win the field.

Canzonets à 4 (1598), xvi

When the tenor voice moves into its uppermost register between bars 22 and 26, some difficulty may be experienced at first in maintaining an even balance, especially where the same figure occurs (at the same pitch) in the alto, as in bar 23. Careful rehearsal and listening will, in the end, improve matters; though the often angular nature of the tenor part must simply be negotiated as smoothly as possible. The references to Vulcan and his broad-minded wife are not without parallel in the music.

77

15   THE CURTAIN DRAWN

GILES FARNABY

    The curtain drawn, I saw my love lie sleeping;
      Thrice happy was that peeping.
      For viewing her sweet lying
  Preserves my life and keeps my soul from dying.
  Of thousand joys, missing her, I had missed all,
  Whose sight revives me more than ruby, pearl, and crystal.

Canzonets (1598), xi
The original underlay is suspicious at many points, and has here been changed to conform with
a more natural association of words and music, notably at bars 11-13, 17, 20-24.

16 APRIL IS IN MY MISTRESS' FACE

THOMAS MORLEY

April is in my mistress' face,
And July in her eyes hath place.
Within her bosom is September,
But in her heart a cold December.

Madrigals à 4 (1594), i

The word July should be stressed on the first syllable. Over-subtle attempts at vocal expression of the four seasons are clearly out of place in such a short and simple madrigal, yet a slight holding back on the melisma of 'September' and a more deliberate tempo (assisted by 'white' tone-colour) for the last line may serve to enhance the character of the performance as a whole. Morley probably took the idea from Vecchi's setting (1587) of Livio Celiano's poem *Nel vis'ha un vago Aprile*, where the first of nine verses presents a clear parallel.

17   DIE NOW, MY HEART

THOMAS MORLEY

Die now, my heart, from thy delight exiled,
Thy love is dead, and all our hope beguiled.
   O Death, unkind and cruel,
   To rob the world so
   Of that her fairest jewel!
Now shoot at me and spare not,
   Kill me, I care not!
O think not, Death, alas thy dart will pain me;
Why shouldst thou here against my will retain me?
   O hear a doleful wretch's crying,
   Or I die for want of dying.

Madrigals à 4 (1594), xix
Careful attention to declamation and timbre will be found to heighten the meaning of this brief but passionate threnody, which may even have been in the nature of an occasional composition. For once the play on 'dying', usually amatory if not downright erotic, occurs here in deadly earnest.

18 NOW IS THE GENTLE SEASON; THE FIELDS ABROAD

THOMAS MORLEY

Now is the gentle season freshly flowering,
To sing and play and dance while May endureth;
And woo and wed, that sweet delight procureth.

The fields abroad with spangled flowers are gilded,
    The meads are mantled, and closes;
        In may each bush arrayed, and sweet wild roses.
The nightingale her bower hath gaily builded,
        And full of kindly lust and love's inspiring,
'I love, I love,' she sings, hark, her mate desiring.

Madrigals à 4 (1594), ix-x

It would be a pity to force the tempo of this pleasant and leisurely pastoral: the requisite life and lightness should come from a springy phrasing closely allied to the sense of the words and the pulse of the music. A long pause between the two parts is not necessary, for the verse forms an entity even though the two musical halves offer distinct evidence of contrasted styles.

19

SAY, GENTLE NYMPHS

THOMAS MORLEY

Say, gentle nymphs that tread these mountains,
    Whilst sweetly you sit playing,
    Saw you my Daphne straying
Along your crystal fountains?
    If so you chance to meet her,
    Kiss her and kindly greet her.
Then these sweet garlands take her,
And say from me, I never will forsake her.

Madrigals à 4 (1594), xx
Some of Morley's poets use 'while' as a conjunction instead of 'whilst', and in view of this it
might be permissible for the sake of euphony to change the beginning of line 2.

-ing, sweet - ly sit play - ing, whilst sweet - ly

-ing, sweet - ly sit play - ing, whilst sweet - ly

-ing, sweet - ly sit play - ing, whilst sweet - ly

-ing, sweet - ly sit play - ing, whilst sweet - ly

you sit play - ing, Saw you my Daph -

you sit play - ing, Saw you my Daph - ne, saw

you sit play - ing, Saw you my Daph - ne,

you sit play - ing, Saw

-ne, saw you my Daph - ne,

you my Daph - ne, saw you my Daph - ne, saw

saw you my Daph - ne, saw

you my Daph - ne, saw you my Daph - ne, saw

my sweet Daph - ne stray - - ing A -

you my Daph - ne, stray - - ing A -

you my Daph - ne, stray - ing A -

you my Daph - ne, stray - ing A - long your

103

20

MY PRIME OF YOUTH

JOHN MUNDY

My prime of youth is but a frost of cares,
  My feast of joy is but a dish of pain,
My crop of corn is but a field of tares,
  And all my goods is but vain hope of gain.
The day is past, and yet I saw no sun;
And now I live, and now my life is done.

In deep distress to live without delight,
  Were such a life as few I think would crave.
In pangs and pains to languish day and night,
  Were too too much for one poor soul to have.
If weal and woe will thus continue strife,
A gentle death were good to cut off such a life.

Songs and Psalms à 3, 4, 5 (1594), xvii–xviii

These two madrigals undoubtedly belong together, since the keys agree as well as the metre and rhyme-scheme of the verses. The first verse comes from a poem said to have been written by Chidiock Tichborne on the eve of his execution in 1586, when Anthony Babington and his fellow-conspirators were unpleasantly put to death for planning to assassinate Queen Elizabeth and others of her household. Alison and East also set the first verse to music, following it by a second verse different from the one used by Mundy.

cares, My feast of joy is but a dish of

cares, My feast of joy is but a dish of

cares, My feast of joy, my feast

cares, My feast of

pain, my feast of joy is but a dish of

pain, my feast of joy is but a dish of of

of joy is but a dish of

joy is but a dish of

pain, My crop of corn is but a

pain, My crop of corn, My

pain, My crop of corn is but a field of

pain, My crop of corn is but a field

field of tares, but a field, a field of tares,

crop of corn is but a field of tares, And

tares, but a field of tares,

of tares, is but a field of tares,

I think would crave.

think would ___ crave, as few I think would ___

few I think would crave, as few I think ___

think would ___ crave, as few I ___

In pangs and pains to

crave, as ___ few I

would crave.

think would ___ crave. In pangs and

lan - guish day and night,

think would ___ crave. In pangs and

In pangs and pains to lan - guish ___

pains to lan - guish day and night, to ___

in pangs and pains to lan - guish day and

pains to lan - guish day and night, and

___ day and night, day and

lan - guish day and night, day and

21 AMYNTAS WITH HIS PHYLLIS FAIR

FRANCIS PILKINGTON

Amyntas with his Phyllis fair in height of summer's sun
Grazed arm in arm their snowy flock; and scorching heat to shun
Under a spreading elm sat down, where love's delightments done,
'Down dillie, down,' thus did they sing, 'there is no life like ours,
No heaven on earth to shepherd's cells, no hell to princely bowers.'

Madrigals and Pastorals I à 3, 4, 5 (1613), vii
Since Pilkington's poet had his tongue in cheek while penning this naughty satire, a correspond-
ing attitude may be emulated in the musical performance, which should in any event sound
light-hearted and extrovert. A slight drop in dynamic level for the words 'thus did they sing'
may be found effective in both repeats of the final couplet.

sing, 'There is no life like ours, no life like
sing, 'There is no life like ours, no life like
sing, 'There is no life like ours, no life like
sing, 'There is no life like ours, no life like

ours, No heaven on earth to shep-herds'
ours, _____ No heaven on
ours, _____ No
ours, _____ No heaven on earth, no

cells, to shep-herds' cells, to shep-herds' cells, No
earth to shep-herds' cells, No
heaven on earth to shep-herds' cells, No
heaven on earth to shep-herds' cells, No

hell to prince - ly bowers.' bowers.'
hell _____ to prince - ly bowers.' bowers.'
hell to prince - - - ly bowers.' bowers.'
hell to _____ prince - ly bowers.' bowers.'

22   HAVE I FOUND HER?

FRANCIS PILKINGTON

Have I found her? O rich finding!
  Goddess-like for to behold,
Her fair tresses seemly binding
  In a chain of pearl and gold.
Chain me, chain me, O most fair,
Chain me to thee with that hair.

Madrigals and Pastorals I à 3, 4, 5 (1613), xi
This poem was set again by Bateson in his 1618 publication. A fairly leisurely, relaxed tempo may be found most suitable for the proper projection of the verse and its thought; bars 15-17 should be tested for balance where the two middle voices change places.

seem — ly bind-ing In a chain of

seem — ly bind — ing

seem — ly bind — ing In a

seem — ly bind — ing

35

pearl and gold, in a chain of pearl and

chain of pearl and gold, of pearl and

In a

gold, in a chain of pearl and

In a chain of pearl and gold, in a chain

gold, in a chain of pearl and gold,

chain of pearl and gold, in a chain of

40

gold, pearl and gold, in a chain of pearl and

of pearl and gold, in a

of pearl and gold, in a

pearl and gold, in a chain of pearl and gold,

23 PALAEMON AND HIS SYLVIA

FRANCIS PILKINGTON

Palaemon and his Sylvia forth must walk,
Of passions past and divers things to talk.
He sighs, she weeps, they kiss, and both complain,
And both of them would something utter fain.
But voice and words were to them both denied,
For they had nought to say that was not said.

Madrigals and Pastorals II à 3, 4, 5, 6 (1624), xi
The word 'sighs' introduces the customary rests, since the Italian word 'sospiri' had this secondary meaning, and English madrigalists were quick to take it over as part of their veiled vocabulary. Let the diction of the almost tongue-tied lovers make its natural effect wherever possible. Tenor and bass underlay have been slightly changed between bars 11 and 13.

125

24 WHAT THOUGH HER FROWNS?

FRANCIS PILKINGTON

What though her frowns and hard entreaties kill?
I will not cease to love, affect her still.
Still will I love her beauty, hate her scorn,
Love her for beauty at her beauty's morn.

Madrigals and Pastorals I à 3, 4, 5 (1613), xii
The text suggests a clear scheme of dynamic levels, but it is important not to over-emphasize
them at the expense of the shape of the work as a whole.

25   WHY SHOULD I GRIEVE?

FRANCIS PILKINGTON

Why should I grieve that she disdains my love,
  Or seek for love, since love's a grief?
A noble mind his tortures ill behove.
  He spoils, thralls, murders like a thief,
  Debarring beauty's bar all loved relief.

Madrigals and Pastorals I à 3, 4, 5 (1613), ix

A sustained opening and quiet singing will most effectively set the mood of this madrigal, whose poetical reference to 'debarring' prompts the observant Pilkington to a musical pun that should certainly be audible, even if invisible.

26 ADIEU, SWEET AMARYLLIS

JOHN WILBYE

Adieu, sweet Amaryllis,
For since to part your will is,
O heavy tiding,
Here is for me no biding.
Yet once again, ere that I part with you,
    Amaryllis, sweet, adieu.

Madrigals I à 3, 4, 5, 6 (1598), xii
Virgil's shepherdess has rarely appeared in so attractive a guise as here, and in spite of the obvious limitations in texture Wilbye has aimed at and achieved a most moving and memorable composition, which should be sung with due regard to key words and ideas. The change of key at bar 36 implies no hesitation in the rhythmic flow of the music.

27   AS MATCHLESS BEAUTY

JOHN WILBYE

> As matchless beauty thee a phoenix proves,
> Fair Leonilla, so thy sour-sweet loves.
> For when young Acon's eye thy proud heart tames,
> Thou diest in him, and livest in my flames.

Madrigals II à 3, 4, 5, 6 (1609), xv
According to one version of the legend of the phoenix, the eagle-like bird sought immolation on the funeral pyre at Heliopolis, a new young phoenix arising from the ashes. The poet's analogy with human love may be a little strained, but Wilbye takes full artistic advantage of what is offered. The suspensions and resolutions at 'sour-sweet loves' should be carefully planned and tuned.

28 LADY, WHEN I BEHOLD THE ROSES

JOHN WILBYE

Lady, when I behold the roses sprouting,
　　Which clad in damask mantles deck the arbours,
　　And then behold your lips where sweet love harbours,
My eyes presents me with a double doubting.
For, viewing both alike, hardly my mind supposes
Whether the roses be your lips, or your lips the roses.

Madrigals I à 3, 4, 5, 6 (1598), x
The poem is a translation of Angelo Grillo's *Quand'io miro le rose,* set by Marenzio (Book VIII à 5) and others. Wilbye found it sufficiently attractive for a second setting (this time for six voices) in his 1598 book, and at least two more Elizabethan translations existed, one of them appearing in Farnaby's *Canzonets* of 1598. The singular verb after 'My eyes' is correct according to sixteenth-century usage, when a pair of eyes was considered a unit. Rests have been added to bars 1 and 6 to assist in breathing and also to preserve the broadly-flowing triple metre. The basic pulse should not change at bar 11. In the final repeat, the upper two voices ought really to exchange parts, but if this makes bars 48-49 too high for the alto there is an easy solution.

29 THUS SAITH MY CLORIS BRIGHT

JOHN WILBYE

Thus saith my Cloris bright
When we of love sit down and talk together:
'Beware of Love, dear,
Love is a walking sprite,
And Love is this and that,
And O I wot not what,
And comes and goes again, I wot not whither.'
No, no, these are but bugs to breed amazing,
For in her eyes I saw his torchlight blazing.

Madrigals I à 3, 4, 5, 6 (1598), xi
Wilbye here has recourse to a translation in *Musica Transalpina* (II, 21) of a madrigal by
Marenzio, *Dice la mia bellissima Licori*, based on a poem attributed to Guarini. The mock
seriousness of the girl's warning is perfectly mirrored in Wilbye's choice of texture, and deserves to be a feature of any really lively performance of this miniature masterpiece.

155

wot not what, and O I wot not

wot not what, and O I wot not

wot not what, and O I wot not

wot not what, and O I wot not

what, And comes and goes a - gain, I wot not

what, And comes and goes a - gain, I wot not

what, And comes and goes a - gain, I

what, And comes and goes a - gain, I wot not

— whi - ther, and comes and goes a - gain, I wot not

whi - ther, and comes and goes a - gain, I wot not

wot not whi - ther, and comes and goes a - gain, I

whi - ther, and comes and goes a - gain, I wot not

— whi - ther.' No, no, these are but bugs to

whi - ther.' No, no, these are but bugs to

wot not whi - ther.'

whi - ther.' No, no, these are but bugs to

breed a - maz - ing, No, no, these

breed a - maz - ing,

No, no, these are but bugs to

breed _____ a - maz - ing, to

are but bugs to breed a - maz - ing, _____

No, no, these are but bugs to breed a - maz -

breed a - maz - ing, to breed a - maz -

breed a - maz - ing,

For _____ in her eyes

For in her

- ing, For in her eyes I saw

For in her eyes I saw his

I saw his torch - light blaz - ing.

eyes I saw his torch - light blaz - ing.

his torch - light blaz - ing.

torch - light blaz - ing.